Is My Lollipop in Heaven?

Is My Lollipop in Heaven?

TYREESE R. MCALLISTER

purposely
created
PUBLISHING

IS MY LOLLIPOP IN HEAVEN?

Published by Purposely Created Publishing Group™

Copyright © 2021 Tyreese McAllister

Printed in the United States of America

ISBN: 978-1-64484-320-8

Special discounts are available on bulk quantity purchases by book clubs, associations and special interest groups. For details email: sales@publishyourgift.com or call (888) 949-6228. *For information logon to:* www.PublishYourGift.com

This book is dedicated to my daughters,
N'Daja Lyndze and Ayana Jazmyn (6/10/1998– 3/21/2017),
and all other children who struggle to understand
the loss of life at the hands of someone else.

"Do you think God has time to read Lolli a bedtime story?" Daja asked her father.

Daddy had been sitting on the edge of Daja's bed reading her a bedtime story, but she hadn't been paying much attention. She had so many questions that would not leave her mind.

Daddy smiled and said, "Yes, I think God has time to read to Lolli. You know how much Lolli loved her bedtime stories."

"I miss her so much," Daja said.

"I know," Daddy replied. "I miss your sister too."

"Daddy, how could someone be so mean and kill kids?"

With tears in his eyes, Daddy said, "I don't know, but me and Mommy have been thinking that we need to take you to someone who will have some answers. Is that okay?"

"Yes, Daddy," Daja said.

One week later, Mommy told Daja that on Wednesday they were going to take a ride into the city to see a therapist. Mommy explained that a therapist is someone you talk to when you're having a hard time dealing with your feelings.

"Are you still sure you want to go?" Mommy asked.

Daja said, "Yes, Mommy. I'm sure."

When Wednesday came, Mommy and Daddy picked Daja up from school. They took the train to a tall building with an elevator that went all the way up to the twentieth floor. When the elevator stopped, they got off, turned right, and walked into a room with lots of cool pictures on the walls and chairs that were placed in a circle.

As Mommy let go of Daja's hand, she looked down at her and whispered, "You've got this. Be brave!"

"We'll be right outside the door waiting for you," Daddy said.

Daja stood frozen for a minute as she watched her mommy and daddy leave the room. Then, she sat down in the pink chair with a butterfly on the back and kicked her feet nervously.

She looked around as other kids got dropped off by their parents and sat down.

First, the boy with the blue shirt sat in the blue chair. His name tag said Nigel.

Daja guessed that he picked the chair that was his favorite color just like she had.

Second, a boy named Diego sat in the green chair across from her.

A few minutes passed, and then a girl with purple ribbons in her hair sat down in the chair next to Daja's. Her name was Courtney.

Then, in came a boy named Zyir, a boy named
Michael, and two girls who looked like twins.
Their name tags said Jazmyn and Lyndze.

As the kids looked around at each other, Daja could
tell that they were nervous and sad just like her.

Ever since Ayana had died in a school shooting two
months ago, Daja was the saddest she'd ever been in her
whole eight-year-old life. Ayana was shy and sweet, and
Daja hated that her sister was dead because of what she
heard her mommy say was "senseless gun violence."

Now, Daja was here with these other kids, waiting for
the person who could help her make sense of it all.

As she squirmed in her chair, a lady with a beautiful red dress walked into the room smiling.

Daja recognized her. She had been in the hallway talking to all the moms and dads.

"Hello," she said. "My name is Dr. McAllister, but you can call me Dr. Mac. I'm really glad that all of you are here today. I know that some of you might be a little nervous, but there is no need to worry. You've been through a tough time from losing someone you love, and this is a safe place to share your feelings. Please introduce yourself and tell everyone who you lost. Who would like to go first?"

Dr. Mac looked around for a volunteer.

When no one raised their hand, Daja figured she should go. Her sister had been the shy one, not her.

"My name is Daja, and someone killed my sister, Ayana. We called her Lollipop, or Lolli, for short."

"It was very brave of you to go first, Daja. I'm sorry for your loss," Dr. Mac said. "Now, who's next?"

The twins held hands.

"I'm Jazmyn. I'm Lyndze," they said at the same time. "Our dad got really mad at our mom last year, and he killed her."

"I'm very sorry to hear that!" Dr. Mac said kindly. "I know that must be very hard for both of you."

Dr. Mac looked around the circle for who would go next.

Finally, Diego said, "My older brother was shot by a police officer after being pulled over in his car."

"I'm so sorry, Diego," said Dr. Mac with a warm voice.

"My uncle committed suicide," Michael blurted out, "and we were very close."

Before Dr. Mac could say anything, Courtney spoke up and said, "Daddy was supposed to be home in fifteen minutes, but he never made it. A drunk driver crashed into his car when he was on his way home from work. They said Daddy died on the way to the hospital."

Dr. Mac looked from Michael to Courtney and told them both how sorry she was.

There were only two kids left to introduce themselves, but they both looked scared.

Daja remembered how she used to help her sister when she was afraid to talk to people. She decided that she would help Zyir and Nigel too.

"It's okay to talk," she said, looking at them. "Dr. Mac said this is a safe place. Plus, all of us have already done it and we're okay."

She looked around for support as the other kids
nodded, and Dr. Mac beamed at her proudly.

Daja felt great to be able to help them
like she used to help Lolli.

The room was quiet for a few minutes, and then
Nigel spoke. His voice was almost a whisper,
so everyone had to lean in to hear him.

"Six months ago, my mom had to go to her second
. . . uhhhm . . . I can't remember the word."

"It's okay, Nigel, sometimes I forget words
too," Dr. Mac said and smiled. "Your mom
was on her second deployment. Can you
explain to everyone what that means?"

"Yes," said Nigel. "Deployment is when people in the
military go away to fight for our country. She said she'd
come home just like she did the last time, but she didn't."

Nigel balled up his fist and punched his
chair when he was done talking.

"Take a deep breath, Nigel," Dr. Mac told him. "I know you're angry. We all understand."

Nigel did as Dr. Mac said and took a few deep breaths. He seemed to calm down after that.

Everyone's eyes turned to Zyir.

He pushed his glasses up on his face and said, "I know we're all sad and mad, but feeling that way won't change anything. It won't bring back the person we lost."

"That's very true, Zyir," Dr. Mac said.

She looked around the circle and said, "What happened to your loved ones was not fair. And like Zyir said, you have been left hurt, sad, and sometimes even mad. And you have the right to be. But we're here so that you won't keep hurting."

She smiled at Zyir and told him to go on.

"It's only been one month since my grandfather was murdered. He saw a man stealing a woman's purse and tried to stop him. The man pulled out a gun and shot my granddad. Killed him on the spot. I miss my PopPop every day. What I told y'all was what he told me after Granny died. I guess it helped him and it sure helps me. I hope it helps all of you too."

"Thank you for sharing some of your grandfather's wise words with us, Zyir," Dr. Mac said as she looked around the circle. "I do hope that what Zyir shared is something that you all will remember. And I have a few other tips you can use when you get sad or mad about losing your loved one. Doing these things will help you to deal with your pain, sadness, and anger. These things will also help you honor your loved one's memories. Do you all understand?"

Daja spoke up.

"I don't really understand what you mean by 'honor your loved one's memories.' Can you break it down for us?"

Dr. Mac smiled and said, "Sure. What I mean by that is, I want to help you be your best even though they are not here."

Daja and the other kids nodded their heads that they understood.

"So, when you're feeling sad or mad, remember that L-O-V-E is the answer."

"Does that stand for something?" Jazmyn and Lyndze asked at once.

"Yes, it does," Dr. Mac said.

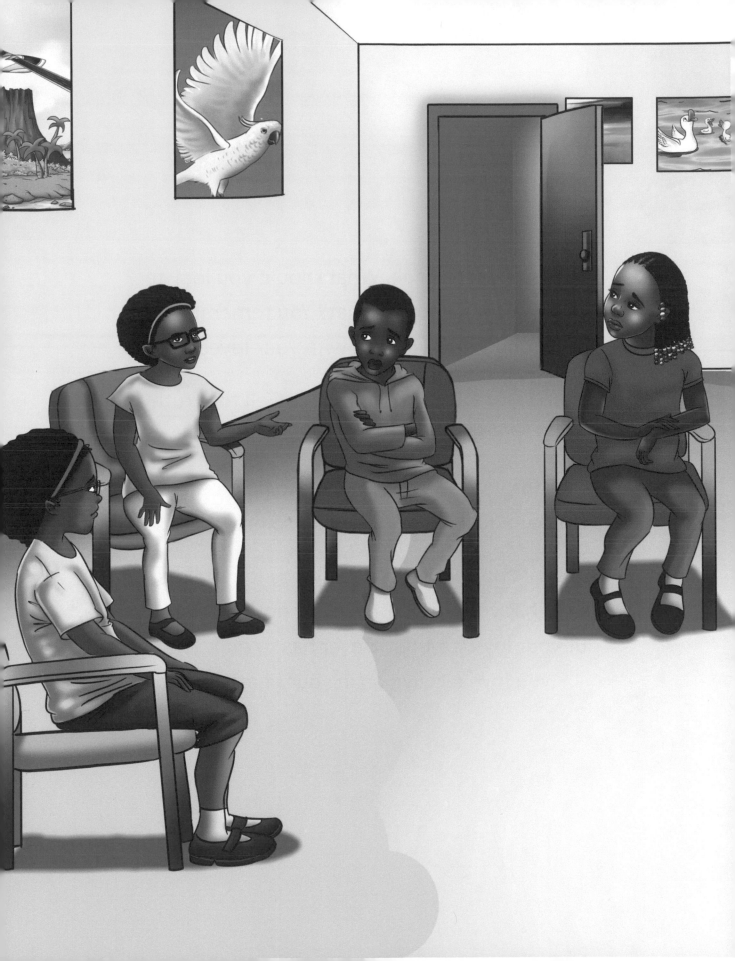

"L stands for Look. What should you look for? Joy. How do you do that? You remember the good times you had with your loved one.

O stands for Own your emotions. Tell the truth about how you're feeling. That way someone can help you.

V stands for Voice. Use your voice to help others deal with their pain. Just like you all were so brave to do today.

And last but not least, E. E stands for Endless. That means that your loved one might not be alive anymore, but your love for them never has to end. The person you love can live on in your heart forever."

There was a knock at the door as soon as Dr. Mac finished talking. She stood up, walked to the door, and told the parents it would be just a few more minutes. Then, she closed the door and walked back to her seat in the circle.

She looked around at us again and asked, "Do you all think you will be able to remember to L-O-V-E?"

In unison, everybody said, "Yes, I will!"

"That's great!" Dr. Mac said. "I am so proud of each and every one of you for sharing your feelings today. Next week, I'm going to teach you all ways to process—which means deal with—your feelings. I look forward to seeing each of you again soon. I will let your parents know we're done for the day."

Dr. Mac walked back to the door and let the parents in. Daja said goodbye to the other kids as she left the room. When she walked outside with her parents, the sun seemed like it was shining brighter than she'd seen it shine since her Lollipop went to Heaven. She grabbed her mommy's hand and squeezed it three times, which meant "I love you." Her mom squeezed it back four times, which meant "I love you more."

Daja was surprised that Mommy knew her
and Lolli's secret hand squeeze.

How did Mommy know it?
Daja thought to herself briefly.

Then she thought, It doesn't matter.

She walked with her parents to the
train with a smile on her face.

"Are you okay?" Mommy asked,
looking down at Daja.

"Yes, Mommy," Daja answered,
"I know how to L-O-V-E now, and
I'm gonna make Ayana proud!"

About the Author

Tyreese R. McAllister is a licensed mental health practitioner with over twenty-five years of experience in the field of emergency mental health, helping individuals who have experienced crisis and traumatic events to recover and overcome through radical resilience. While Tyreese's work experience gave her the knowledge to write a book about therapy, it was the murder of her eighteen-year-old daughter, Ayana, and her inability to find a book that explains homicide to children that led her to write a children's book, *Is My Lollipop in Heaven?*

Tyreese earned her master's degree in counseling psychology and a postmaster's certificate in addictions counseling from Johns Hopkins University. She is a bestselling c-author of Soul Talk, Vol. 3. Tyreese has also coauthored a book with her husband, Anthony Jerome, *Fathers Matter: Changing the Narrative of Black Fathers.* They both reside in Upper Marlboro, Maryland.

Learn more at www.tyreesemcallister.org

CREATING DISTINCTIVE BOOKS
WITH INTENTIONAL RESULTS

We're a collaborative group of creative masterminds
with a mission to produce high-quality books to position
you for monumental success in the marketplace.

Our professional team of writers, editors, designers,
and marketing strategists work closely together to ensure
that every detail of your book is a clear representation
of the message in your writing.

Want to know more?
Write to us at info@publishyourgift.com
or call (888) 949-6228

Discover great books, exclusive offers, and more at
www.PublishYourGift.com

Connect with us on social media

@publishyourgift

CPSIA information can be obtained
at www.ICGtesting.com
Printed in the USA
BVHW051505220421
605631BV00002B/136